The Bell Tower

Martyn Beardsley

Illustrated by Sholto Walker

Ginn

CHAPTER 1

The Room Next Door

Lizzy Dean sat in the back of the car with her arms folded across her chest and a grumpy look on her freckled face.

"Aren't you getting out, Lizzy?" asked her dad, whistling cheerfully.

That only made it worse, Dad whistling cheerfully. They had just arrived at their holiday cottage on a farm in Wales. Lizzy wasn't even sure where Wales was, and she certainly didn't want to be there. She wanted to be in Devon or Cornwall where they usually went, where there were amusement arcades and loads of things to do.

"Ooh, look!" cried Mum. "How lovely!"

A long row of whitewashed cottages stood before them.

"That must be the Bell Tower," said Mum, "which means we're in the cottage on the left."

Exploring her temporary new home lifted Lizzy out of her mood a little. She rushed upstairs to pick the best bedroom before Mum and Dad could stake their claim.

"This one!" cried Christopher, turning left at the top of the polished, wooden staircase. He climbed onto the smaller of the two beds.

At the far end of the room was a door. Lizzy decided to find out where it led to.

"What in it? What in it?" demanded Christopher, bouncing on "his" bed.

"Hang on! I haven't even opened it yet." Lizzy tried, but the door was locked. There was a large keyhole beside the handle, and she bent down, closed one eye, and peered through with the other. All Lizzy could make out was a bed that looked much older than the ones in their room.

Lizzy wandered over to the open window and leaned out. To her left she could see the window of the room next door – the Bell Tower room. She could see the bell high above her, and wondered if it still rang.

Lizzy decided two things as she gazed down at her parents unloading the car. Firstly, the locked room must belong to the next-door cottage. Secondly, there was something mysterious about it.

Opposite the cottage, the ground sloped quite steeply downwards, and beyond a line of rather skinny trees Lizzy could see the grey, slate roof and upper rooms of a very big house. It was clearly an ancient place. The walls, that had once been white like the cottages, were now grey, patchy and cracked like the skin of an old man.

Lizzy spotted a woman of her gran's age making her way up the path from the big house. At the same moment, the sun peeped out from behind rippling white clouds and lit up the scene like a spotlight. Lizzy's heart lifted a little more when a dark-haired boy, just a little younger than herself, came running along behind the woman. A grizzled old brown dog waddled at his heels, struggling to keep up.

Lizzy ran downstairs (her trainers squeaking on the shiny staircase) and out into the sunshine.

Lizzy's parents and the woman were having the usual sort of boring grown-up talk: "Had a good journey?" … "Weather's not bad, but it could be better" … "At least it's not raining". Lizzy's mum told the woman all their names.

Looking at Lizzy, the woman announced, "My name's Janet Llwellyn, and this here is Thomas, my grandson. He'll be glad of two new playmates!"

"I've got an electric car that you can really drive," beamed the boy proudly. His strong Welsh accent was peculiar, but fascinating to Lizzy's ears. "You can have a go – but not too long or the battery runs out."

Lizzy had thought it would be nice to have someone to play with, but she'd already got Thomas down as being both a bit of a show-off, and a bit bossy.

"Thanks," she replied, as if to say "I'll let you know".

"Are you going to tell them about Uncle Gareth?" Thomas asked his gran.

"Don't be silly, Thomas," she quickly replied, and then she said something in a whisper to the boy, which Lizzy guessed must have been in Welsh. She was still smiling, but she looked irritated.

"Does the bell in the tower still work?" Lizzy asked.

Thomas sniggered, and now Lizzy was really annoyed. It wasn't such a daft question, was it?

"Hasn't worked for donkeys' years, dear," replied Mrs Llwellyn. "Anyway, I have to be getting on. If there's anything else you need, you might find me down at the big house. If I'm not there, there's my husband, Max – though he's usually out on the farm somewhere. See you later!"

Their first sight of Max Llwellyn came later that day when they were returning from a short walk, exploring the grounds before dinner. As they trudged up the path back to their cottage, they saw a solitary figure sitting on a low wall, staring up at the Bell Tower. He was old and hunched, with a leathery, outdoor face.

He sat as still as a statue, gazing at the building as if waiting for something to happen.

He didn't even notice them walk by, and Mum said, "Shall we go and introduce ourselves?"

Dad shook his head. "Later. Looks like he's got something on his mind."

That night, tired from the journey, they all went to bed early. But Lizzy couldn't get to sleep. First there was Christopher:

"Lizzee!"

"What?"

"Are you 'sleep?"

"Shush!"

"But Lizzee!"

Then there were the other voices.

Somebody must have moved into the cottage with the Bell Tower, because every now and then, just as she was nodding off, Lizzy would hear low, muffled voices from the room next door.

There was a child's voice, maybe a boy. He sounded tearful and upset. Lizzy couldn't make much of it out, except he kept coming back to something about chasing "Sam" …

And then there was the bell.

In the middle of the night, Lizzy was woken from a deep sleep. It was one of those times when you're not sure whether the thing that woke you was in a dream or real. But she felt sure she had heard the bell ring for real. She could still hear the echo in her mind.

Lizzy climbed wearily out of bed, went over to the window, and peeled back the curtains. It was as if she had woken to find herself in a cottage at the edge of the universe. Lizzy was used to living in a town, where it never got completely dark, what with all the streetlights, house security lights and so on. But out here, deep in the countryside, it was so black it seemed

that there was only nothingness beyond
the window.

As Lizzy turned to go back to bed,
thinking that she must have been dreaming
about the bell after all, there was a sound
that nearly made her jump out of her skin.

Someone was trying the handle of the
door between her room and the Bell Tower.
And this time she wasn't dreaming.

Lizzy dived back into bed and pulled the covers right up underneath her nose. If someone came in, they might not notice her in the dark if she kept perfectly still – even though the sound of her breathing itself seemed loud enough to give her away.

But the handle didn't rattle again, and Lizzy remembered that the door was locked. Probably someone sleepwalking, or forgetting which way to go to the toilet. It was the first night of the holiday, after all ...

CHAPTER 2

Voices in the Night

The following morning, billowing white clouds sailed majestically through a big, blue sky. The events of the previous night seemed far away, but Lizzy couldn't wait to ask her parents if they had heard the bell ring. They both said they were so tired after the journey that they had been dead to the world.

"I hear bell!" declared Christopher earnestly – but Lizzy was sure he was pretending, just to impress everyone.

After breakfast, the Dean family took a trip to Castell Henllys, an iron-age hill fort from the really old days when people lived in smoky huts and painted themselves blue. A lady dressed in iron-age clothes painted Lizzy's and Christopher's faces with blue patterns, but Christopher kept rubbing his until he ended up looking like someone had thrown a paint pot at him. Lizzy enjoyed the fort, and began to think that Wales wasn't such a bad place after all.

The family arrived home late in the afternoon. While Mum and Dad flopped on the sofa with a cup of tea, Lizzy was allowed to go and look at the garden and lake at the front of the big house, as long as she stayed away from the water.

Lizzy made her way down the steep path, between the sun-dappled orchard on her right and the big house on her left. She came to a neatly mown lawn at the front of the house. It sloped down to a sundial and some stone steps, which in turn led to a large field with the lake at the bottom – a shimmering patchwork of reflected greens, blues and whites. Two white geese waddled along the water's edge in single file, making a noise as if they were complaining about something or other.

"Fancy a game of footy?" came a voice from behind, which made Lizzy jump. It was Thomas, carrying a ball.

"Okay." Lizzy said.

Thomas threw the ball to her, and they began to kick it back and forth between them.

"Who do you support?" Thomas asked. "I support Manchester United."

"But you live in Wales!" exclaimed Lizzy.

"So? I can still support them, can't I? They're the best," said Thomas, proudly as he gave the ball a powerful kick.

"I know – I support them as well."

"Are you from Manchester, then?" asked Thomas.

"Well, no ..." replied Lizzy sheepishly, realising she had talked herself into looking rather silly. But when Thomas laughed and said, "See!", Lizzy joined in, and they both made each other giggle more and more.

Thomas made a goal out of some stones, and Lizzy tried to shoot the ball past him. When it was her turn to go in goal, Thomas blasted the ball so hard that Lizzy spent more time getting out of the way than trying to save it. Show-off! she thought – though now she was getting to know him she decided he wasn't so bad … Then she remembered how he had laughed when she'd asked Mrs Llwellyn if the bell in the Bell Tower worked.

"Anyway, that bell does ring," she announced grandly.

"Does not! The little ringing thing inside's all rusted up."

"I heard it last night. I'm in the room right next to it – and someone from next door tried to come into my room by accident in the middle of the night. I'm glad the door was locked!"

Thomas, who was just about to take a

mighty whack at the ball, stopped himself and put his foot on it, frowning. "There's nobody staying in the cottage next to you."

"There must be. Someone tried to open the door – and I heard someone talking," explained Lizzy.

"Let's go and see!" Thomas suddenly seemed excited.

As Lizzy ran up the steps and crossed the lawn after him, she thought it was odd that someone who must be used to holiday-makers coming and going all the time should get worked up about such a little thing. It might be just that he was eager to prove her wrong, but Lizzy suspected that it was because Thomas knew something about the Bell Tower that he was keeping from her.

Their trainers raised little puffs of grey dust as they scurried up the stony path towards the cottages. Standing in front of the archway, Thomas pointed up at the bell

triumphantly. "Look – it's all rusty
and stuck."

"It might be able to ring a bit in the wind,"
argued Lizzy – though she secretly felt that it
looked highly unlikely, now that she could
see it properly.

Thomas was pressing his nose against the
window of the cottage on the other side of
the archway. "Empty. Told you!" He tried the
door handle. It was locked.

Lizzy shielded her eyes and gazed in. There were no signs of life whatsoever.

"Then who was it?" Lizzy wanted to know.

Thomas looked around as if to check whether anyone could hear them. "I bet I know – but I'm not allowed to tell …" he said.

"What do you mean?"

Just then they were interrupted by Lizzy's mum calling her in for dinner.

"Are you playing later?" Lizzy asked.

"Yeah! Get your mum and dad to bring you down to the big house. There's a bar and a room to play in." And then, because he could tell that Lizzy was still wondering about the Bell Tower, Thomas looked up at the empty bedroom. "You can try asking Gran or Grandad about the Bell Tower room – but don't say I said anything."

CHAPTER 3

The Boy in the Boat

That evening, Lizzy and her family went inside the big house for the first time. Mrs Llwellyn showed them some of the rooms before they went to the bar. The place seemed vast compared to their cottage, with high ceilings and old paintings and ornaments everywhere. It reminded Lizzy of a stately home she had visited on a school trip.

There was another couple in the bar with two children who were quite a bit older than Lizzy and didn't take much notice of her. But everyone got on well, and Mr Llwellyn was serving the drinks. He was much more cheerful than when Lizzy had seen him before, making everyone laugh with his funny stories. Dad started to tell his very unfunny jokes, and though Mum groaned and pestered him to stop, Mr Llwellyn kept egging him on.

Lizzy wanted to ask Mr and Mrs Llewellyn about the Bell Tower, and the secret that Thomas had hinted at. She looked at Thomas, and he seemed to know what was on her mind and gave a quick shake of his head. Lizzy thought it was probably because there wasn't really any secret at all.

But in the night, Lizzy heard the mysterious voice again.

She found herself half-awake, half-asleep, staring up at the shadows on the ceiling, awoken by what she thought was the sound of the door handle from the Bell Tower. Had it been a dream, or even a memory of last night coming back to her in her drowsy state? Either way, she could certainly hear the boy's voice, tearfully pleading, and a jumble of words and sobs, which always came back to that name "Sam", "Sammy …"

Lizzy's first thought was that Thomas was playing a trick on her, but she soon dismissed that. It didn't really sound like him, and anyway, she didn't believe he could put on such a good act. The boy in the Bell Tower room was very upset about something. She climbed out of bed as quietly as she could so as not to wake Christopher, and crept to the door.

" … chasing him … Looking for Sammy! Not your fault. Never your fault!"

Plucking up her courage, Lizzy whispered as loudly as she dared, "What's the matter? Can I help you?"

The voice in the other room stopped, and everything was suddenly so quiet and normal that Lizzy felt quite stupid to be talking to herself.

There were no more sounds that night.

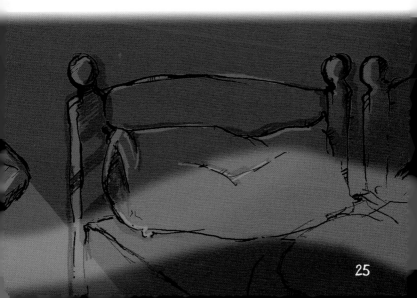

At breakfast, Mum and Dad planned what they were all going to do that day. First they would go to a theme park with rides and all kinds of fun things. Christopher had seen a leaflet about it on the day they had arrived, and had been going on about it ever since. Rain was forecast for the afternoon, so they decided to go to a chocolate-making factory, and Lizzy was hoping for some free samples.

Before it was time to set off, Lizzy and Christopher wandered outside. The old dog struggled up from his resting place by their car and waddled over to see them.

"Hello, Benji!" Lizzy greeted him. As soon as she started to stroke him, he rolled over on his back, wagging his tail.

"Is doggy dead?" Christopher asked, squatting down for a closer look.

"Don't be silly – look at his tail. That means he likes it!"

Christopher kept putting his pudgy little
hand near the dog's belly to stroke it like his
sister, but each time his courage would fail
him. "Doggy bite me ... "

Lizzy heard the sound of a car engine and
tyres scrunching through the gravel. She
looked up to see Mr Llwellyn in his Land
Rover, rolling to a halt.

"Morning, you two," Mr Llwellyn said. "Old Benji'll let you do that all day. Where are you off to today, then?"

Lizzy told Mr Llewellyn their plans, and then, almost without thinking about it, she looked up at the bell and added, "Does it work, that bell? Only, I thought I heard it the other night."

"Nah," Mr Llewellyn replied. He had a faraway look in his eyes, as if the question had sent his mind off to an unexpected place, and Lizzy remembered seeing him sitting staring up at the room.

She sensed that he didn't want to talk about it, but her desire to find an answer to the mystery got the better of her. "And I keep hearing a voice in the room next to mine – the Bell Tower ... "

Mr Llewellyn shook his head. "All locked and empty, young lady. Must have been that fox that keeps coming round – they make some funny noises, you know."

Lizzy saw Thomas appearing from around the back of the Land Rover. He must have heard some of the conversation, and he gave her the same sort of look that he had last night, as if to say "Don't". But she knew full well it wasn't a fox (whatever they sounded like). "It was a boy, and he was talking about someone called Sammy."

Mr Llewellyn suddenly went very pale. "Sammy, you say?"

"Yes." She noticed Thomas watching his grandad's reaction, almost as if he was afraid.

Mr Llewellyn chuckled. "Hah! That old fox!" But as he revved the engine and went on his way, Lizzy could see the grim expression on his face.

Thomas watched his grandad leave, his hands deep in his pockets. "How did you know about Sammy? Tell me, Lizzy," he demanded.

"Because that's what the boy was talking about," Lizzy answered back.

"Gran told you, didn't she?"

"No," Lizzy replied angrily. "I heard the boy in the Bell Tower room say it, and I know I heard the bell ring! What's going on, Thomas?"

Thomas began pulling faces as if he was trying to decide whether to tell her or not. "I'm sorry. I can't say. I'd get in really big trouble."

And that was all Lizzy got out of him.

They had a great day out. Christopher got soaking wet in the bumper boats and happily went round wearing Dad's sweatshirt like a long dress for a couple of hours, and Lizzy was picked out during a demonstration to decorate some chocolates in front of loads of people. Lizzy decided that Wales was as good as Devon and Cornwall, if not better!

But as soon as they got back, there was

only one thing on Lizzy's mind – to find Thomas and work on him until he told her his big secret. She was sure he was close to cracking. Had they got someone locked away like a prisoner for some reason? She couldn't imagine Mr and Mrs Llwellyn doing anything like that, but she'd heard stranger true stories on the telly …

A light drizzle was falling as Lizzy walked down to the front of the big house. Looking across the field to the lake, she thought she could see Thomas out on the water in the little rowing boat, which was normally left tipped upside down on the grass. But as Lizzy got closer, it began to dawn on her that it wasn't Thomas at all. She decided to turn back. The rain was getting heavier … and … and … there was something about the boy in the middle of the lake, staring at her through the misty curtain of drizzle, something strange. Something that frightened her …

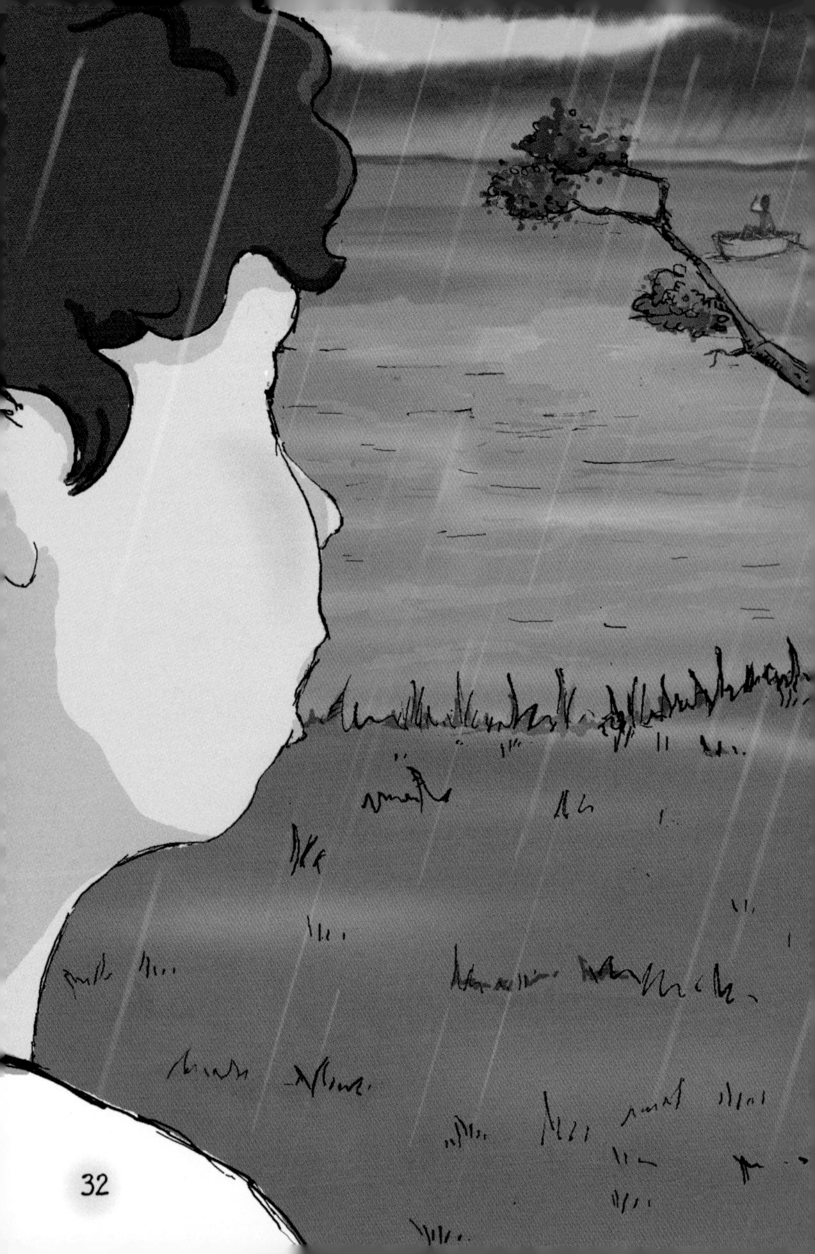

Just as she was about to go, the boy waved. Lizzy gave a half-hearted wave back as she turned and trotted up the lawn towards the house. She doubted whether he saw it, and feeling she'd been rather rude, she turned back to give a proper wave. But the boat was upside-down on the grass at the edge of the lake, and there was no sign of the boy.

With a shiver, Lizzy hurried back up the path to the cottage.

CHAPTER 4

Thomas Shares a Secret

When Lizzy got back to the cottage, a delicious smell of cooking greeted her nostrils and made her realise how hungry she was. Dad was doing something on his laptop computer when Mum called to him.

"Can you come and give me a hand with the veg, Alan?"

"Sure," he said. He was about to switch the machine off, but Lizzy piped up, "Can I play a game on it?"

Dad left it out for her. "Okay – but dinner's in ten minutes. Don't start moaning when you have to leave the game before you've found the gold in the lost caves of Peru, or whatever it is."

Lizzy laughed. She sat down at the coffee table where Dad had been working. The laptop was in word processor mode, and it looked like he had left some unfinished work on it, which was not like him.

"Dad!" Lizzy called, not wanting to get into trouble for losing something important. But then her voice trailed away. The cursor was blinking at the end of a short message, which seemed to be for her.

"What is it, Lizzy?" Dad called back.

"Oh, nothing. Er ... did you save your work and go back to the desktop?"

"Yes. Is there something wrong with it?"

"No ..." Lizzy was staring really hard at the computer screen now.

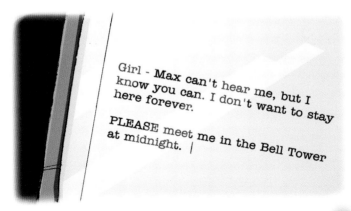

Girl - Max can't hear me, but I know you can. I don't want to stay here forever.

PLEASE meet me in the Bell Tower at midnight. |

"I don't believe you!" said Thomas when he heard Lizzy's story that evening. They were sitting under a tree at the edge of the lake. Lizzy repeated what had happened, and had all but given up trying to convince him that she had heard the voice and there had been a message for her on the computer, when he seemed to have a change of heart. Although he didn't go so far as admitting she might be right, Thomas began to tell her a story …

"My mum told me that Grandad Max had a brother who died when they were both little. His name was Gareth, and he died in a fire. Grandad was really upset about it – anyone would be, but he was especially upset, because he thought it was his fault. Gareth was the youngest, and Mum says he once ran out of the stables absolutely petrified because he'd heard a strange noise. It was probably just a rat or something, but

after that, Grandad always used to tease him about being scared. He used to pretend there was a monster in there, to wind Gareth up."

"One day, there was a big fire in the stables. Nobody realised that Gareth was inside until it was too late. Grandad thought Gareth must have gone to the stables to prove that he was brave, because he'd got so fed up with all the teasing. Grandad believes Gareth knocked over one of those old lanterns with a flame inside and that's how the fire started. Mum says Grandad never got over it. He'll never talk about the fire to anyone, and he'll never allow anyone in the room where Gareth died."

"Where were the stables?" asked Lizzy.

"The stables were changed into the cottages where you're staying. And the room where they found Gareth's body ... it was ..."

Lizzy gasped. "The Bell Tower!"

"Yes. I'm coming with you tonight, Lizzy."

There he goes, being bossy again, Lizzy thought. "What makes you think I'm going anywhere in the middle of the night?"

"We've got to!" insisted Thomas.

Lizzy had never seen him looking so serious. "Have you got the key?" asked Lizzy.

"We won't need one,"

Lizzy was confused. "How do you know?"

Thomas explained to Lizzy, "Well, one night, I heard the voice like you did. The door was locked, I know it was, but at midnight it suddenly opened!" Thomas hung his head in shame. "I was too scared to go in – but it'll be better if there's two of us. I'll meet you in your room at midnight."

"We could get into big trouble!" Lizzy warned, not wanting to mention how afraid she was at the thought of meeting a ghost.

"If we don't do something now, this could go on forever!" explained Thomas. "I want to do it to help poor Grandad. He pretends to be cheerful, but he's not – not really."

Lizzy liked Mr Llwellyn too, and couldn't help feeling sorry for Gareth, if that was his ghost stuck in the Bell Tower. "Be careful, and be quiet!" said Lizzy. "I'll see you at midnight, then."

CHAPTER 5

Midnight in the Bell Tower

Lizzy heard an owl calling from one of the trees outside her bedroom window, then a distant answering call from somewhere in the woods beyond the lake.

She checked the luminous dial of the clock beside her bed for the umpteenth time. Funny, she thought, that when she wanted to get to sleep she couldn't because of all the mysterious noises, but when she wanted to stay awake it was a struggle to stop herself nodding off.

She eased herself off the bed. Earlier, once Christopher had fallen into his usual deep, unbreakable slumber, she had put back on her jeans and T-shirt and had been lying in them ever since.

After what seemed like an age, Lizzy heard the sound of footsteps on the polished wooden stairs. She tensed, afraid that Thomas was making much too much noise. The silence of the night was so deep that every tiny sound seemed to echo throughout the cottage. She could even hear Thomas holding his breath and then having to let it all out in a rush, like a lemonade bottle being opened.

Light appeared in the gap at the bottom of the bedroom door. The door slowly opened, and a torch-beam waggled around the room until its strong white light found Lizzy's face, making her shield her eyes.

"Have you heard anything?" Thomas asked in a whisper.

"No. Shall we try and go in?" It was easy to say, but the very thought of going into that room gave Lizzy the jitters.

Thomas pointed his torch at his wristwatch. "It's not midnight yet, but we might as well. I don't suppose ghosts have watches … " He was trying to sound cool, but there was a tremor in his voice.

They followed the beam of the torch to the door handle. Taking a deep breath, Lizzy grasped it. The cold metal sent a shiver like a small electric shock through her hand and into her arm. Her breath came in short, jerky bursts, and a small, fretful part of her hoped it would stay locked.

Lizzy turned the handle half-way, and shook her head. "It won't – "

She stopped in mid-sentence. At first it had definitely felt locked. Now, the handle was suddenly loose in her hand, and the door slowly inched ajar, opening up a daunting, black chasm.

"I don't think this'll work if you use the torch," Lizzy warned. She took her first step into the doorway, hardly able to believe what they were both about to do. Thomas switched off his torch and followed her into the midnight darkness of the Bell Tower.

"Can't see anything so far," Lizzy remarked in a fearful, hushed tone. She could barely even make out Thomas, standing right beside her.

"Sshh!" came the reply. Nevertheless, she felt his arm reaching out for her, and they held onto each other to boost their flagging courage.

As their eyes became accustomed to the darkness, they began to see certain shapes around the room: the bulk of the bed, the outline of a large dressing table, and a full-length mirror showing the dim reflection of one of them.

At least, it looked like a reflection …

Lizzy stared hard at the shape in the mirror. Something about it didn't look right. She raised an arm.

The reflection didn't move.

She nudged Thomas and he turned to see what it was she wanted. Still no movement from the figure. An icy-coldness came over Lizzy, and her skin tingled as if a thousand insects were crawling along her spine and up her neck.

She knew it was him.

"What do you want?" Lizzy asked in a whisper. Even the thin sound of her own voice seemed scary.

Thomas gripped Lizzy's arm tighter. "What do you mean, what do I want?" whispered Thomas.

Then came the other voice.

"Max?"

Lizzy and Thomas cowered together, struck dumb with fear. This was no longer an exciting adventure. A real ghost stood before them. A real ghost knew they were there, and wanted something from them. It was not an image in the mirror, but a boy. A small, silvery pale figure shimmering in the blackness, like a moonbeam come to life. He was tearful and sniffling.

"Why did you take so long, Max?" the ghost cried.

"He thinks you're Max," whispered Lizzy.

"I couldn't go without letting you know.
It wasn't your fault. Understand, Max?"
The ghost's mournful, little pleadings would
fade and return, like a radio not properly
tuned into the station. It seemed to be
seeping from the walls around them,
lingering in the darkest corners, a sorrowful,
whispering breeze.

"N-not really ... " stammered Thomas.

"It weren't about no monsters like you
thought! Nothing to do with your old teasing!
It was Sammy, the old devil – ran inside.
Couldn't let him burn, could I?
Understand, Max?"

"Well ... " Thomas began falteringly. He
had no idea who Sammy was or what he had
to do with anything. But the flickering figure
of Gareth Llwellyn was beginning to fade
away. He seemed to know his chance was
nearly over, and reached out his thin arms

to them.

"Say you understand ... Please say it's all right now!"

Gareth's ghost was almost gone. All that remained was a misty outline in the blackness and some weepy, feeble and distant words. They could feel his pain, his heartbreak, as if they were taking it in with every breath. Lizzy felt tears gathering in her eyes.

Thomas seemed to be frozen to the spot, unable to reply. Lizzy gave him a sharp jab with her elbow.

"Yes!" blurted Thomas. "Everything's okay now!"

But his voice was swallowed by the dark and empty room. The unhappy ghost of Gareth Llwellyn had gone, and Lizzy and Thomas had no idea whether their scary, midnight adventure had achieved anything at all.

CHAPTER 6

Sammy

The next day, stone circles and a castle were on the menu. But Lizzy didn't want to see stone circles and a castle – she wanted to see Thomas and Mr Llwellyn. She prowled around the big house after breakfast, but there was no sign of anyone. She knew that Mr Llwellyn was often out on the farm very early, and that Thomas sometimes went with him to help out.

The Dean family set off in their car, down the long farm track leading to the main road. The sun was doing its best to break through the clouds, but Lizzy didn't notice. All through the night, she had lain awake tossing and turning, wondering whether she and Thomas had done the right thing – whether they had put an end to the misery of the poor, tortured spirit of Gareth Llwellyn.

Suddenly, Dad braked hard, sending them all lurching forward in their seats. They had met a Land Rover trying to turn into the entrance at the same time as they had been swinging out.

"Sorry, folks," murmured Dad as he started to reverse their car to make room for the other vehicle.

But Lizzy wasn't. It was Mr Llwellyn's old Land Rover, and Thomas was inside with him. "Just a minute," she cried. "I've got to get out!"

"Eh?" said Dad, pulling on the handbrake. "Where are you going, Lizzy?"

"I come! I come!" shouted Christopher.

But Lizzy was already bounding up to the Land Rover. "Have you told him?" she yelled through the open window. She could see by the look on Thomas's face that he hadn't. "You've got to!"

Thomas squirmed in his seat.

"What's all this?" asked Mr Llwellyn. "Tell me what?"

"You know I told you I heard the bell ring, and voices in the Bell Tower?" Lizzy began. Mr Llwellyn's smile faded. He even looked a little angry, but Lizzy knew it was now or never, and she pressed on regardless. She decided, however, that it would be easier for him to believe if she didn't quite tell him the whole story.

"I heard the voice again. It said it wasn't your fault."

"I don't know what you're talking about, I'm sure, young lady," replied Mr Llwellyn, but Lizzy could tell he was fibbing. He just didn't want to know.

She took a deep breath and let it all come rushing out before he had a chance to stop her. "It was someone called Gareth. I suppose it might have been one of the farm workers," she added. "He says what

happened – whatever it was – wasn't to do
with you teasing him at all. He only went into
the fire because he was chasing someone
called Sammy, trying to save his life.
Gareth's spirit can only find peace when you
know the truth. He can't be happy until you
are and stop blaming yourself!"

"Grandad, who's Sammy?" Thomas piped up at last.

Mr Llwellyn just stared into space, his hands gripping the steering wheel. It was impossible to tell from his face what he was thinking. The sound of Dad impatiently tooting the horn brought him back to earth.

"Sammy wasn't a who as such, Thomas. He was a dog. A little black-and-white terrier, who was always running off and getting into mischief," explained Mr Llwellyn. He was gazing straight ahead, and it was as if he were talking to himself. "But that was a long time ago ..."

Now it all made sense! Gareth had been trying to rescue his dog from the fire, not trying to prove to his brother that he wasn't afraid to go into the stables. That was why Gareth had to bring an end to Mr Llwellyn's years of guilt and suffering.

But Mr Llwellyn still looked serious, and

he would say no more about it. They went their separate ways, with Lizzy worrying for the rest of the day about whether she had done the right thing or had perhaps even made things worse.

One thing was for sure. There was a different feel about the cottage.

The bell didn't ring again, and Lizzy slept soundly for the rest of the holiday.

On the morning Lizzy and her family were leaving, Mrs Llwellyn and Thomas came to see them off.

Thomas wore a mischievous expression.

"We're opening up the Bell Tower," said Mrs Llwellyn. "Max has suddenly decided that it's a pity not to be able to take a bigger party in the next-door cottage. I don't know what's got into him ..."

Lizzy's heart lifted. She and Thomas exchanged knowing grins. They knew.

And as the family drove away, they saw

Mr Llwellyn. He spotted them and waved cheerily, and although Lizzy couldn't be sure, she thought he gave her a special wink.

"Well, I think we've had a pretty good time," declared Mum as they drove up the hill away from the farm.

"I want to come again next year," Lizzy said.

"You've changed your tune," remarked Dad. "You didn't even want to come to Wales!"

"Well, now I do – and next time I bagsy the Bell Tower!"